Postman Pat® Goes Football Crazy

SIMON AND SCHUSTER

It was a sunny day in Greendale, and everyone was getting ready for the five-a-side football match.

"Come on, Dad!" called Julian, as he jogged past Pat who was wobbling along on his bicycle. "You need to get fit for the game! See you on the playing field!"

At the Post Office Mrs Goggins had a huge pile of letters for Pat.

"Gosh! I'll have to deliver this lot double quick if I'm going to get to the match on time!" Pat sighed.

"Aye, Pat, you don't want to miss that!" smiled Mrs Goggins. "I'll bring along a wee snack for half time!"

Pat loaded up the van and was all set to go – but the engine wouldn't start!

"Oh no!" he groaned. "Looks like we'll have to deliver the post by bicycle today, Jess!"

"Mi-aow!" Jess didn't like travelling in the bicycle basket!

"Hold on tight, Jess. There's no time to lose!"

Pat whizzed along so fast, he didn't see Dr Gilbertson and Sarah jogging towards him.

"Watch out, Pat!" Dr Gilbertson called.

Pat swerved to avoid them, and toppled into the bush!

"Are you ok, Pat?" asked Dr Gilbertson, helping him up.

"I think so! But just look at all my letters. Now I'll be late for the match!"

"That's where we're off to,' said Dr Gilbertson. "We'll help you pick up the post, Pat."

Sarah rescued Jess and gave him a cuddle.

"Miaow!"

Jeff Pringle, Charlie and Julian were already on the playing field. Charlie was busy making notes.

"Shouldn't you be practising, Charlie?" Julian asked.

"I'm just working out the angles of the ball . . ." explained Charlie.

"Right, these sweaters will do as goalposts until Bill Thompson brings the real ones," said Jeff Pringle. "Now, Julian. Give it your best shot! Charlie, which side will the ball go?"

"Hold on, Dad!" cried Charlie, scribbling away in his book. "I'll just work it out . . ."

Julian belted the ball . . .
Jeff dived to try and catch it – and landed flat on his back!

"GOAL!" shouted Julian.

"Ooops!" said Charlie. "You jumped the wrong way, Dad! SORRY!"

At PC Selby's house, Jess was just stretching his legs when there was a deafening whistle. Jess jumped in fright, but with a flying leap, Pat caught him just as he fell from the bicycle basket!

"Good save, Pat!" laughed Lucy, running over, as PC Selby gasped for breath behind her. Lucy blew her whistle again.

"Come on, Dad, up, down, up, down! I'm training him for the match, Pat!"

“I’m not cut out for this,” puffed PC Selby.

“Hmm. With your police training I bet you’d make a great referee, Arthur!” suggested Pat.

“Referee? Now that’s more like it!” grinned PC Selby.

Pat's next stop was Thompson's Ground. He had to weave his way skilfully through a flock of sheep.

"Anybody here?" he called.

"Just looking for the goal posts!" Bill Thompson shouted from inside the shed. "Oh look, here's my old beach ball!"

Suddenly the ball came flying though the air towards Pat. Pat caught the ball with his foot and started doing fancy tricks.

"Hup! Hup! Hup!"

"That's amazing, Pat!" admired Bill, emerging from the shed.

Pat's last stop was the Bains'. He knocked on the door, but there was no one in. Then Pat saw Nisha, Meera and Nikhil heading down the road.

"I'd better catch up with them, Jess. This letter might be important."

Pat jumped back onto his bicycle – but the front tyre was flat!

"Oh no! That's all I need!" he groaned.

Pat raced down the street on foot.

"Here's your post, Nisha," he panted.

"Thanks, Pat," said Nisha.

"Wow! You can run really fast!" said Meera.

Pat pumped up his bicycle tyre, and checked his watch.

"Oh dear! They might have to start without us, Jess!" he muttered, as they set off again.

Meanwhile, on the playing field, everyone was ready for the game.

PC Selby split them into two teams.

"Right, Dr Gilbertson, Sarah, Lucy, Charlie and Jeff can be in one team. And Nisha, Meera, Bill and Julian, you can be in the other team."

"But where's Dad?" wailed Julian. "He's supposed to be in our team. We can't start without him!"

Suddenly Pat sprinted across the pitch.
"You made it, Dad!" Julian cried.
Pat laughed. "Only just!"

PC Selby blew his whistle and the game began! The players passed, tackled, collided, tapped, shot and saved!

Pat ducked, dived, dribbled, swerved, skidded . . .

and SCORED!

"It's a goal! Julian's team wins!" announced PC Selby, blowing the final whistle.

Everyone cheered.

PC Selby presented Julian with the trophy.

"We couldn't have done it without you, Dad," said Julian proudly.

"Yes, Pat. How did you learn to play like that?" asked Meera.

Pat chuckled. "Delivering the post today turned out to be the best football training I could have had!"

"Miaow!" agreed Jess.

SIMON AND SCHUSTER
First published in 2005 in Great Britain by Simon & Schuster UK Ltd
Africa House, 64-78 Kingsway
London WC2B 6AH

Original writer John Cunliffe
From the original television design by Ivor Wood

A CIP catalogue record for this book is available from the British Library upon request

ISBN 0 689 87558 4

Printed in China

3 5 7 9 10 8 6 4